Grandma
Bird

For my two Grans,
for Esther's Nannie
& Nanny,
and for Gladys.

Rock to rock,
Eye to eye,
Side by side,
You and I.
Skimming blue,
Low and high,
I, the sea,
You, the sky.

SIMON & SCHUSTER
First published in Great Britain in 2018 by Simon & Schuster UK Ltd, 1st Floor, 222 Gray's Inn Road, London WC1X 8HB • A CBS Company • Text and illustrations copyright © 2018 Benji Davies The right of Benji Davies to be identified as the author and illustrator of this work has been asserted by him in accordance with the Copyright, Designs and Patents Act, 1988 • All rights reserved, including the right of reproduction in whole or in part in any form • A CIP catalogue record for this book is available from the British Library upon request • Printed in Italy • ISBN: 978-1-4711-7179-6 (HB) ISBN: 978-1-4711-7180-2 (PB) • ISBN: 978-1-4711-7181-9 (eBook) • 10 9 8 7 6 5 4 3 2 1

Grandma Bird

Benji Davies

SIMON & SCHUSTER
London New York Sydney Toronto New Delhi

Noi lived with his dad and six cats by the sea.

It was summer and Noi was going to stay at Grandma's.

It was a long way to Grandma's house.
She lived by herself on a tiny rock where the wind
cut in and the grass grew sideways.

The only visitors were the birds who blew in
and out on the breeze.

Noi wasn't sure about Grandma.

She boiled up seaweed for soup
and kept her teeth in a jar.

At night they had to sleep top to tail.
The blankets were itchy and Grandma snored
like an old walrus.

During the day, Grandma always seemed too busy with one thing . . .

or another . . .

and she never had time to play.

So one morning, when the tide was out,
Noi crept away.

He hopped from rock to rock
and pattered over wet sand.

He dipped in and out
of rock pools.

Then he spotted something
shimmering across the sand.

It was a great big rock full of holes. Noi weaved
in and out and skipped around its edges.

It was a castle, a tall ship, a smuggler's den.
It was the barnacled back of an ancient whale.

Outside, the sky swirled black and grey.
A storm was brewing.

Noi listened as the sea thrashed against
the rocks and rain began trickling down the walls.

Suddenly, with a flutter
and a squawk, something tumbled out
of the storm and landed in Noi's cave.

It was a little bird
and it didn't look well.

The tiny bird shivered
in Noi's hands.

He knew he must
do something, and quickly.

Maybe Grandma would know what to do.

The tide had come in and it was hard to find a path across the rocks. Noi hopped, jumped and leapt with all his might.

But the storm blew him left and right. Noi wondered how he would ever make it back to Grandma's . . .

when suddenly, a sail came cutting
across the sea.

"Grandma!" shouted Noi.
"I've got you!" cried Grandma,
as she scooped them aboard.

"Thank goodness I found you!" she said.
Grandma had started searching for Noi
as soon as she heard the storm.

As they sailed home, Noi and Grandma found more of the windswept birds. "They must have been on a long journey together," said Grandma.

The house was soon full of chatter and the ruffle of drying wings.

Once the storm had passed, the birds went on their way.

Only Noi's bird didn't want to leave.

"I think he likes you, Grandma!" said Noi.

Noi wondered if Grandma ever felt lonely living out here by herself.

They spent the rest of the summer together, exploring every rock and shore . . .

. . . and Grandma's bird came too.

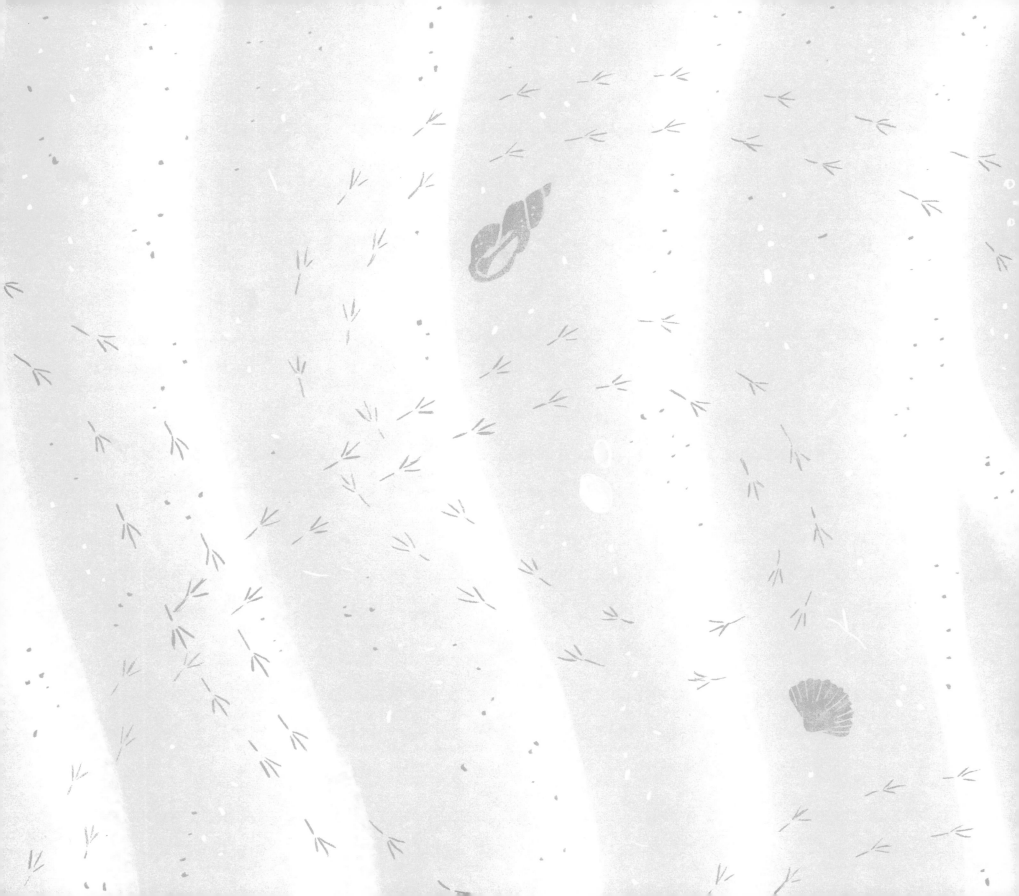